For Gareth, Gerard, Laura,
Caroline and Jennifer
FT

To family and friends
- love always x
ÚH

Published by
PrimaryABC,
Abercorn House,
57 Charleston Road,
Dublin 6, Ireland.

Telephone: + 353 1 269 5008
Email: primaryabc@eircom.net
Web: www.primaryabc.ie

Designed by: Cormac Hanley

ISBN-13: 978-0-9545837-3-6
ISBN-10: 0-9545837-3-6

LOOK WHAT BLEW INTO THE ZOO

Story by Fiona Tierney

Illustrations by Úna Healy

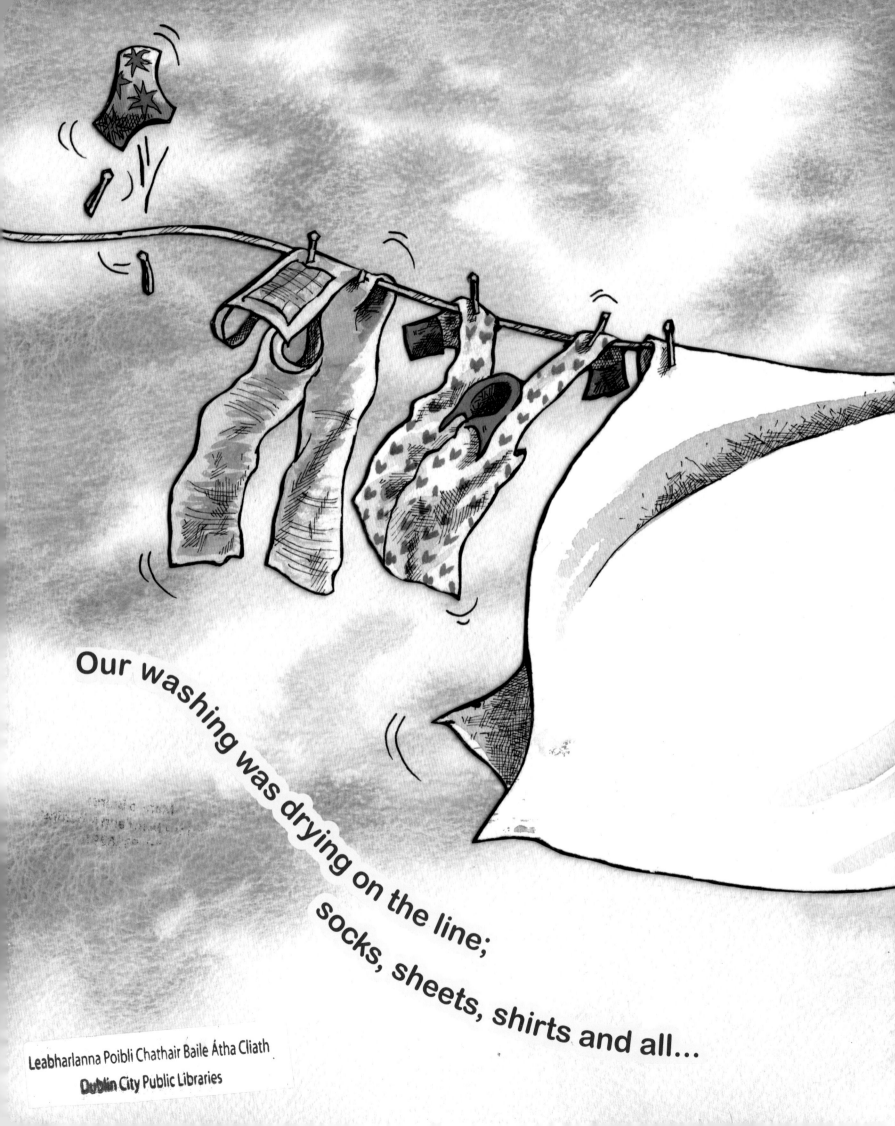

Our washing was drying on the line; socks, sheets, shirts and all...

when a mighty gust set them loose
and over next door's wall.

We were watching from the house
and laughed as off they blew.

"Let's go next door and have some fun"
- you see we live beside the Zoo!

"Oh" sighed the **Elephant**,
"I'm so tired of being grey.
It's just the same old dreary thing
each dull and boring day."

"Look at what's just landed here!
These **pants** will fit me nicely.
They're exactly what I wanted
to change my look precisely."

"But wait a sec, I want a name to match my brand new style.

Elepant sounds good to me", he added with a smile.

Old **Crocodile** was another, feeling lonely, sad and blue.
He went to see the doctor, who told him what to do.

"You need to soften yourself up - you're too scaly, hard and rough.
You'll have to find a way to show, deep down, you're not so tough."

Just then our socks fell from the sky,
croc pulled them on with glee.
He went to look for some new friends...

"I'm a **Sockodile** now you see."

The poor old Chimpanzee was sore,
his knees were red and rough.

Everyone knows that chimps love to climb,
but not that it can be so tough.

"All that climbing is hard on the legs,
as I scramble amongst the trees.

What I need is something hard-wearing,
to protect my poor knobbly knees."

As he was wondering what to do,
he spied where my jeans lay...

The **Cheetah** was feeling chilly,
as she comes from a warmer clime.

"It's not so bad in summer" she said,
"but it's c-c-cold in winter-time."

"By day my fur coat keeps me warm,
but I'd love something extra at night.

Something to wrap around myself.
Something nice and light."

Then out of the blue (or so it seemed),
a **sheet** came sailing past.

She put up a paw and pulled it down...

and was a cosy Sheetah at last.

Kangaroo was rather fed up.
Her kids were causing her stress.

With mud-pies, paint and sticky jam,
they'd made an awful mess.

As if that wasn't bad enough;
she is the kind of mummy,
whose messy kids are carried
in a pouch inside her tummy.

"These look like they could help",
as she pulled on some cool dungarees.

She smiled and kissed her youngsters' heads...

"Nobody seems to think I'm cute",
sobbed the Turtle to her Dad.

"I'm not like a puppy, a kitten or lamb
and it makes me feel quite sad.

I'd love to look nice and pretty,
have earrings and bracelets and jewels.

With fancy clothes, some ribbons and bows,
I'd be queen of the turtle rock-pools."

Mum's best shirt had fallen down,
near where the turtle was sighing.

She slipped it on and looked divine.

"I'm a

so no more crying".

The Owl was feeling grumpy.
He was finding it hard to sleep.

He had flown and hunted all night long
and was trying to count some sheep.

Every time he tried to nod off
he was woken by a sound;
like a roar or a hiss or a mighty yawn
that would echo all around.

His eyes were red and his temper frayed,
when our towel fell over his head.

It helped block out the light and noise

"I'm a Towl" he sleepily said.

Polar Bear wasn't feeling too well.
His throat was rather sore.

The doctor had to take a look,
and told him not to roar.

"At least until your
throat heals up,

which will take
about a week.

You'll have to keep
it very warm

or you'll only be
able to squeak."

When Dad's **polo neck sweater** landed nearby,

he put it on with delight.

"I'm a **Polo Bear**
who can roar all he wants",

and he roared with all his might.

We met the zookeeper as we strolled along,
and he asked if we'd help with the chores.

"The animals are happy today", he said.
"Can you hear how loudly Owl snores?"

"Should we ask for our clothes back?
Should we make a big fuss?

No! The animals seem so happy
and sharing's important to us.

Let's keep this a secret between us,
say nothing so no-one will know…

except for the animals in the **Zoo**
who'll smile when the wind starts to blow!"